My Hood

by Linda Oatman High

ISBN-13: 978-1-68021-130-6
ISBN-10: 1-68021-130-7
eBook: 978-1-63078-462-1

Printed in Guangzhou, China
NOR/1115/CA21501590

20 19 18 17 16   1 2 3 4 5

The **hood**
is not good.

I should
not wear
my hoodie
out in town

This is what
my mom
keeps saying.
"Black boys
get shot," she
says.

"It happens
a lot.
Every day
in the USA.
Shot for no
reason
by the
police.

BREAKING NEWS

Tyrone Lee Jones, 16   Shot on Green Street

"I do not need
to see your name
on TV.
'Tyrone Lee Jones, 16.
Shot on Green Street.'"

I sigh.
Roll my eyes.
Pull up
my hood.

"No way," says Mom.
"Not a good choice.
Don't I have a voice?
Makes you look
like a thug."

I give her a hug.
"I am no thug," I say.

"I know that!" Mom says.
She shakes her head.
Her long dreads
swing.

Mom should have **wings.**

My mom is an angel.
So full of love for her
one and only son.

"But what about
all those police
with their guns?"
she says.

"Nobody will shoot
my son!
Not if I
can help it."

Being the only son
is not always fun.
My mom is one
to *hover*.

She is like a fly.
Or a flea.
She likes to hang
with me.

She seems to forget
I am a teen.
No longer her baby boy.
I am her pride
and joy.
Mom is all about
her son.

"I can run," I say.
"If the police come
after me, I'll run."

Mom play-slaps
my head.
"Can't run when you're
dead," she says.

The List

Michael Brown
Samuel Dubose
Ezell Ford
Kendrec McDade
Tamir Rice
Timothy Stansbury
Christian Taylor

World - Business -

Issue: 240104

First Edition

The list
goes on.
And on.
Mothers' sons
shot by
cops.

I know their names.
Mom says them
when we pray
for their souls.

"Their bodies had bullet holes.
For no good reason,"
Mom says.

"Blood flowed
in the streets.
This old world
can be so
cold."

We live
on Green Street.

You watch
your back
on Green Street.

GREEN ST.

There is a house
for crack.
Every night there's
an **attack.**

Lights are black.

People have a knack
for fights.

Blacks against whites.
Whites **against** blacks.
It sucks.

It is wintertime.
So cold.
My winter coat
is old.
Full of holes.

My hoodie is new.
A present
from Grandma.

"I'm just going to
Yasmen's place," I say.
I pull the hood
to my face.

Yasmen is my best friend.
We've been tight
since we were seven.
She's so smart.

Yasmen has a *good heart*.
She doesn't judge.
Or make fun of me.
She doesn't care.
That I can't read
so well.
Or write.

And Yasmen is white.

"You look ready to fight,"
Mom says.
"Don't think you're always right,
Tyrone Jones.
I can feel it in my bones.

"Wearing that hoodie
is not a good plan.
I don't need to see
you on TV.
Don't want your name
on the list!"

Mom's dark eyes mist.
She gives me a kiss.

"I have a flashlight
on my phone. And I know
how to dial 911.
Your only son
is not dumb.
Plus the moon is
shining bright."

I step out
into the night.

"Yo, Tyrone!" calls out the old neighbor man.

"You should not wear
a hood in the hood!
Always comes to
no good.
When I was young,
we called bad guys
'hoods.' "

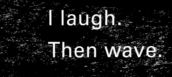
I laugh.
Then wave.

"That was back in the day," I say. "We have come a long way."

He folds his hands
as if to pray.
"We still have a long way
to go, you know."

I am so cold.

I pull the hood tight.

Move forward into the night.

Yasmen is outside.
"Look!" she says.
"Snow!"

It is snowing.
Blowing tiny flakes.
It looks like we
are inside
a snow dome.

It snows.
And snows.
Yasmen is wearing a
white coat.

A cop car floats by.

"Hey!" yells the guy inside.
"Are you okay?"
He is talking to Yasmen.

She gives a thumbs-up.

"Are you sure?" asks the cop.
He stops the car.

I look up at the stars.
Take a breath.
Not ready for death.

The hood goes down.
I am no clown.
Sometimes Mom is right.

I am safe
in the night.

TEEN EMERGENT READER LIBRARIES®

BOOSTERS

The Literacy Revolution Continues with
New TERL Booster Titles!

Each Sold Individually

EMERGE [1]

9781680211542

9781680211139

9781680211528

9781680211153

9781680211122

ENGAGE [2]

9781680211146

9781680211337

9781680211290

9781680211535

9781680211313

EXCEL [3]

9781680211306

9781680211320

NEW TITLES COMING SOON!
www.jointheliteracyrevolution.com